THE SIMPLE PRINCE

JANE
YOLEN

Pictures by **JACK KENT**

Parents' Magazine Press · New York

Text copyright © 1978 by Jane Yolen
Illustrations copyright © 1978 by Jack Kent
All rights reserved
Printed in the United States of America
10   9   8   7   6   5   4   3   2   1

Library of Congress Cataloging in Publication Data
Yolen, Jane H.
    The simple prince.
    SUMMARY: A prince who has tired of his life at court
aspires to lead the simple life, but finds it much
harder than he imagined.
    [1. Princess—Fiction]   I. Kent, Jack, 1920-
I. Title.
PZ7.Y78Si   [E]   78-6118
ISBN 0-8193-0960-5   ISBN 0-8193-0961-3 lib. bdg.

Quite simply—for Marilyn

There was once a prince
who longed to live
a simple life.
He was tired of idle foolishness
and fancy dress balls.

So he clapped his hands
three times to call
his servants.
"Bring me some plain clothes,"
he demanded. "I am going
out into the world
to live the simple life."

The servants found a plain suit
and a plain hat as well.

The prince clapped his hands
three times and ordered
a simple picnic lunch
to eat on his way.

Then he rode off
to find the simple life.

He rode for many hours
until at last he came to
the house of a poor farmer.

"If I cannot live the simple
life here," said the prince,
"then I cannot live it anywhere."

He got off his horse and went
to the door. He clapped his
hands three times. Nothing
happened.

He snapped his fingers.
He tapped his toes.

At last he grew impatient.
"Open up," he ordered.
The door was opened.
The farmer looked out.

"I have come to live
the simple life,"
said the prince.
He walked inside.

The farmer stared at his wife.
She stared at the prince.
The prince did not notice.

Instead he went around the room
with his handkerchief to his nose.
"What an awful smell,"
said the prince.
"Is this what comes
from living the simple life?"

"No!" said the farmer's wife.
"It comes from making cheese."

"Cheese!" said the prince.
He sat down on a stool and
clapped his hands three times.

"I want some cheese. And a cup
of tea to go with it. I have
been on the road so long
looking for the simple life,
I am quite starved."

The farmer looked at his wife.
She shook her head. "No good
will come of this," she said.
The farmer just smiled.

He cut the prince a slice
of cheese. Then he said:
"Cheese and tea. That is
simple. Here is the cheese.

"But as for the tea, we need
fire and water. First I must
saw the wood for the fire.
It is simple. Come with me."

The prince went outside with
the farmer. They found some
wood. They sawed, and they
sawed, and they sawed some more.

The woodpile grew bigger and
bigger. At last the prince
cried out, "Enough! Enough!
I can do no more."

"We are done," said the farmer.

He loaded the prince's arms
with wood and led him back
to the house.

Then the farmer made the fire.
The prince sat down again.
"Now it is time to get the
water," said the farmer's wife.
"It is simple. Come with me."

So the prince followed
the farmer's wife to the well.
Arm over arm, he pulled the
bucket up. He poured the bucket
into a pitcher. One bucket.
Then another. Then a third.

At last the prince cried:
"Enough! Enough! I can do no more."

"We are done," said the farmer's
wife. She gave the prince a
pitcher for each hand. She put
another on his head. Then she
led him back to the house.

The farmer's wife poured the
water into the kettle and put
the kettle on the fire. When it
was hot she made the tea.

But the prince was twice
as hungry as before.

The prince clapped his hands
three times. "Bring me some
bread and butter with my tea."

"That is simple enough,"
  said the farmer.
"But butter begins with milk,
  and milk comes from a cow.
  Come along with me."

So the prince followed
the farmer to the barn.
There he held the pail
while the farmer milked the cow.

The cow's tail hit the prince's
face. The cow's hooves kicked
the prince's knees. At last
the prince cried "Enough! Enough!
I can do no more."
"It is done," said the farmer.

Back in the house, the farmer
made the prince churn, and churn,
and churn the milk into butter.
When it was done, the prince
fell back on the stool.
He clapped his hands feebly
three times. "My butter
needs some bread," he said.

"That is simple," said the
farmer's wife. "But first we
must bake it.
Come along to help."

So she rolled up the prince's
sleeves and gave him
a big lump of dough.

He kneaded it.
He patted it.
He punched it.
At last he cried "Enough! Enough!
I can do no more."

"It's done," said the farmer's
wife, and she put the dough
into the oven to bake.

But the prince was so tired from
sawing and hauling,
from milling and churning,
from kneading and pounding,
that he fell fast asleep.
He slept through
the bread-baking
and dinner, and did not
wake up until morning.
He felt stiff and tired and
cranky. He tried to clap
his hands—one time, two times,
three times. But his hands were
much too sore from all the
work he had done.
"Please," he said weakly,
"may I have something
to eat?"

"It's simple," the wife began.
But before she could finish,
the prince jumped up from
the stool. "Enough! Enough!"
he cried. "I can live no more
of the simple life. It is
much too hard for me!"

He ran out the door,
climbed on his horse,
and galloped back to the castle
as fast as he could go.

His servants helped him
off his horse, and
the grateful prince said,
"Thank you."

Then he asked,
"Please, may I have
some porridge.
I am quite starved."

His servants rejoiced at being
treated so politely and went
quickly to fetch the porridge
and a pitcher of fresh milk.

And from that day to this,
the prince lived happily,
never again clapping his hands
for anything.

Instead, he was always careful
to say "please" and "thank you".
It was so much simpler that way.